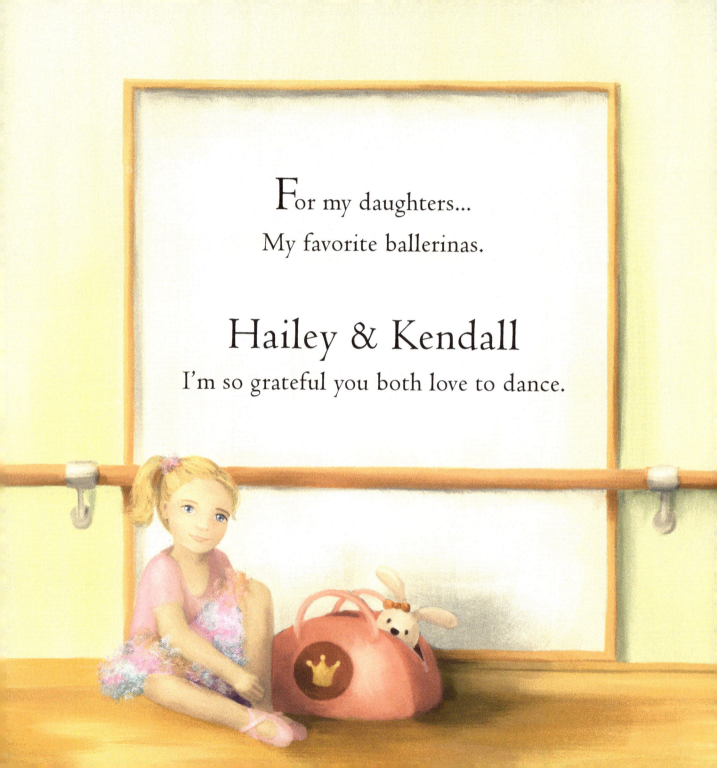

For my daughters...
My favorite ballerinas.

Hailey & Kendall
I'm so grateful you both love to dance.

You are my dreams come true.

XO, Mama

See if you can find
the 7 images of Ballet Bunny,
Miss Juju's favorite toy!

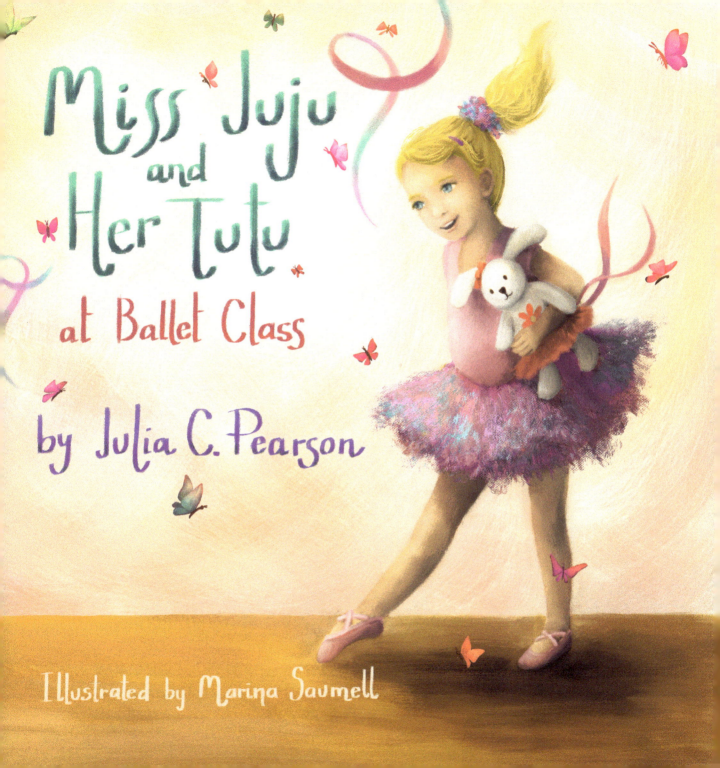

Miss Juju
and
Her Tutu
at Ballet Class

by Julia C. Pearson

Illustrated by Marina Saumell

Miss Juju loves to dance,
She dances every day,
She puts her tutu on
And practices ballet.

Mama tells Miss Juju,
"Today's your favorite day!"
"Ballet class? Oh, could it be?"
Miss Juju shouts, "Hooray!"

First she checks her tutu,
With pinks, purples and blues.
Then Mama puts her hair up
And she grabs her ballet shoes.

Music fills the hallway,
Teacher opens the door.
"Time to dance!" She sings,
Juju skips out to the floor.

Sitting close together,
Today they're butterflies.

Nose to toes and stretches,
Graceful arms float to the skies.

Across the floor she's careful,
Miss Juju likes this part.
Airplane arms and lifted chin,
Don't drop the ballet heart.

At the barre she listens,
And pliés quietly.
Kissing knees and tummies in,
She giggles excitedly.

Chassé on the yellow line,
Skips with knees up high.

Arabesque super straight,
Ballet class is flying by.

Pixie dust and lipstick,
Tiara and pointed toe.
Dreaming of the day
She has her first solo.

Purple ribbons fill the air,
Free dance is so much fun!
Miss Juju twirls in her tutu,
So happy to leap and run.

Cheers for the parachute,
Up and down the colors go.
Teacher says to shake it fast,
Then go high and low.

It's time to say goodbye,
Teacher blows a kiss.
Mama claps her hands,
This is ballet bliss.

Miss Juju loves to dance,
Oh, what a special day.
Now she dreams of tutus,
So thankful for ballet.

I ♥
Ballet

THE 5 BALLET POSITIONS

1st Position

2nd Position

3rd Position

4th Position

5th Position

THE 5 BALLET POSITIONS IN PLIÉ

1st Position

2nd Position

3rd Position

4th Position

5th Position

Meet the Author
Julia C. Pearson

Julia C. Pearson has been a dance instructor and director for more than 20 years. Her passion for dance and love for the classroom has inspired hundreds of little girls and boys to practice ballet.

Mrs. Pearson is a 3rd generation ballet teacher, following in the footsteps of her mother and grandmother. Along with ballet, writing has been an easy favorite for the author all her life. She has a B.A. degree in English Literature from SDSU and a Master of Arts in Organizational Leadership from Regent University. She has dreamed of writing a book series for children and Miss Juju and Tutus is truly a fantasy becoming reality.

Mrs. Pearson lives with her handsome husband and darling daughters in beautiful San Diego where she teaches dance at Danceology Performing Arts Campus. You can Find Mrs. Pearson on Instagram @JuliaPearson.

Trust in the Lord with all your heart!

Proverbs 3:5

Special Thanks

All Glory to God for the creative idea of Miss Juju. Special Thanks to Carl Pearson, Marc & Kathy Ong, Jerry & Tami McKinney, and Niki Lucia for a lifetime of unwavering love and support. Much gratitude to Geoff Hopf, Mary Jenson, and Marina Saumell for their professional guidance.

CLAIM YOUR FREE GIFT!

Visit ➡ PDICBooks.com/Gift

Thank you for purchasing

Miss Juju and Her Tutu: at Ballet Class,

and welcome to the Puppy Dogs & Ice Cream family.

We're certain you're going to love the little gift
we've prepared for you at the website above.

CPSIA information can be obtained
at www.ICGtesting.com
Printed in the USA
LVHW071204220222
711713LV00004B/114